"*My Last Na*... story. With a generous heart and sure sentences, Schumacher gives us an entire life in these few pages, a life we come to care about, and which, though it's a difficult one, is not without its blessings."

— Bret Lott, National Council on the Arts appointee, NYT best-selling author, Oprah's Book Club selection

"This novella might be the most psychologically honest, narratively engaging, and spiritually beautiful thing I have read this year. The words from these pages haunted me long after I read them, and moved me to gratitude, wonder, and even joy. The word that comes to mind as I read this story is 'life.' Read it and see: what it kindles in you will enliven you."

— Russell Moore, author of *The Courage to Stand*

"In *My Last Name*, Schumacher has crafted a tender, sensitive, and quietly lyrical portrait, infused with a bright, longing ache. This exploration of the expansive interior life of an elderly character near death, reminds us that we are all living in the middle of stories — stories that are going somewhere. His readers are likely to feel some gentle tug of the eternal vicariously drawing their own hearts along."

— Douglas Kaine McKelvey, author of
The Angel Knew Papa and the Dog

"*My Last Name* by Eric Schumacher is a poignant reflection on life and dignity. In a single day of an elderly narrator, her life unfolds as she remembers key moments from her past with sharp clarity, even though she's restrained by the unreliable physical trappings of old age. In crafting a story that slides effortlessly between the past and the present with subtle symbolism and careful juxtaposition, Schumacher demonstrates the value of each moment of our lives, and the inherent worth of every person who enters—and exits—our individual narratives."

— K. B. Hoyle, award-winning
author of *The Gateway Chronicles*

"I have probably written more than a hundred endorsements over the years. And I've meant every one of them. But I've never felt as inadequate as I do right now in trying to explain how important this writing is or how moved I was in reading it. But that's how I feel about this novella from my friend, Eric Schumacher. This is a beautiful story written by a poet who has thought deeply about aging and loss and redemption and the hope of the risen Christ. It's an honor to add my name to it. Seriously."

— Elyse Fitzpatrick, author of *Home*

"Eric Schumacher is a gifted writer, clear and generous, and full of soul."

— S.D. Smith, author of *The Green Ember* series

"Eric Schumacher offers a deep and gentle reminder that everyone's life tells a story. What's more, there's a story behind our stories."

— Ruth Buchanan, author of *Unseasonable*

"Eric Schumacher invites readers into an assisted living unit and introduces us to Lottie, who is drifting slowly between periods of cognitive decline and moments of clarity in the last movement of her long life. Lottie's past and present unfold in this remarkable novella with unflinching dignity. The grace of Schumacher's spare and shimmering writing make *My Last Name* a story readers won't soon forget."

— Michelle Van Loon, author of *Becoming Sage*

"As Charlotte Marie struggles to remember her name, we discover she is not unacquainted with suffering, loss, pain and heartache. We are introduced to 'Lottie' as an old woman who has survived everyone and everything. Her journey is one that resonates deeply with the experiences of many women. *My Last Name* is powerful, poignant and beautifully written. Eric Schumacher has given us a gift."

— Christine Caine, author of *Undaunted* and founder of A21 and Propel Women

Other Titles by Eric Schumacher:

Worthy: Celebrating the Value of Women
with Elyse Fitzpatrick

MY LAST NAME

ERIC SCHUMACHER

In memory of my grandparents,

Carl and Verna Schumacher

Leonard Blinn and Charlsie Pickett

Truly the light is sweet,
and a pleasant thing it is
for the eyes to behold the sun.

— Ecclesiastes 11:7

The knocking at the door wakes me. I must have dozed off.

"Who is it?" I try to mutter, but no sound comes out. I clear my throat and try again.

A girl dressed in pink pajamas opens the door and enters. *Who is she? Should I know her?* I don't recognize her. I close my left eye to look with my right. My left eye only sees colors and light and dark and shapeless forms.

The girl in pink pajamas walks to my bedside. Now I see. She is not wearing pajamas. Those are hospital clothes. *Am I in the hospital? Have I hurt myself?*

The girl is slender, but her shirt stretches slightly across her stomach. She is not a girl, but a young woman—soon to be a mother, I think—with light skin, hazel eyes, and thick amber hair pulled back into a ponytail. That smile. It's so sincere—familiar, as though she knows me. *Think, old woman—who is she?* No, I do not remember her.

"It doesn't look like you've eaten much. Are we not hungry this morning?" Her voice sounds familiar, lilting as it does when one speaks to a child. "Would you like me to take your tray?"

Maybe she can tell me where I am. Who I

am… But I can't get these words from my mind to my mouth. I try, but they won't come. So I close my mouth and smile at her and nod and look out the window at the sparrows as she removes the tray.

"Are you feeling okay this morning, Lottie?"

Lottie. That is my name. Short for Charlotte. I am Charlotte Marie. Marie was my mother's name. I am Charlotte Marie…*hmm*…Charlotte Marie something.

"Mrs. Barnes?"

The young woman in pink is looking at me.

"Are you feeling okay, Mrs. Barnes?"

Barnes. Yes, that is my last name. And now, it's all there. I chuckle to myself. It *is* my last name. But it is also my *last* last name—Charlotte Marie Barnes. I have had more than one last name. Barnes was not my *first* last name, but it will be my *last* last name; I will not have another name. That I know.

If I am Mrs. Barnes, then there is a Mr. Barnes. No, there *was* a Mr. Barnes.

As though by habit, I touch the ring on my left hand. A small band of silver, with a diamond chip too small to sparkle. I could not take that off now if I wanted to—not over that gnarled, arthritic knuckle. It will go to the grave with me, like my last name.

My *last* name. I chuckle again.

"Well, it's sure nice to see a smile, Lottie." The young woman in pink laughs. "Do you want to sit in your chair this morning?"

"Yes, that would be nice." The sound of my voice—quiet, frail, old—surprises me.

The air in the room feels cold as she pulls back my blankets. It is colder still as she helps me change from my pajamas into my clothes for the day.

There is a name badge clipped to her front pocket—Sarah. Her name is Sarah.

As Sarah helps me to the chair next to the window, the sparrows scatter at our movement. They will return. There is still seed on the snow. There are always more sparrows.

"Would you like your lap blanket, Lottie?"

"Yes, thank you." The voice of the old woman speaking surprises me again.

"There," she says, tucking the blanket around my legs and over my feet. "How is that? A warm lap blanket is always nice on a cold day."

I smile at her and at her kindness.

"Anything else I can get for you, Lottie?"

"No," I answer. "I'm fine."

"Okay then." Her warm fingers rest on my hand. It feels good to be touched. "I'll check on you a little later. But if you need anything, just press your button, okay?" She places a hand on my chest, on something on my chest. She lifts a small plastic box with a big square button on a cord that hangs around my neck. "You remember, Lottie, you just push that button if you need me, okay?"

I remember for a moment and smile and nod.

As she walks to the door, I am stirred by the sudden need to ask her something. I try to speak, but I cannot remember her name. So I stay silent. The young woman in pink opens the door and leaves. The door closes behind her.

I cannot remember now what I wanted to ask her, the young woman in pink pajamas.

Zig-zagging stripes of yarn, alternating between sky blue and cream. The young woman in pink called it a lap blanket, but it is not a lap blanket. Well, it is a lap blanket now. But it was not made to be a lap blanket.

I sat in the living room with... with... *You ought to be ashamed of yourself, Charlotte Marie Barnes! They cared for you—both of you—in those days and in the days to follow, more than you ever could or did repay.* What were their names?

Mom and Dad. That's what I called them then; they asked me to, and I wanted to. Perhaps that's why I can't remember their names. I always called them Mom and Dad. *Mom and Dad...*

My! I cannot remember their last name now either. And that's bad! Their last name was my last name! Well, my *second* last name.

We sat in Mom and Dad's front room in the old farmhouse. There was a small fireplace, which Dad would tend as Mom rocked and I worked on my first crochet project. Mom taught me to crochet to keep me occupied in the evenings while Dad snored. Together we waited and worried. Sometimes we just wept.

I was slow at first. Who am I kidding? I was always slow. I was not raised to do handiwork. I was raised on the tough work of tending animals and carrying loads and wrestling with my brothers and avoiding my father.

The blanket grew as my belly grew, and it was done when Jack was born.

Jack was born in the upstairs of that farmhouse in February, on my birthday. I was eighteen years old.

February. It is February. There, on the end table next to my chair, is a greeting card shaped like the number 95. It reads "Happy Birthday" at the top.

Yes. I am ninety-five. It is 1995.

I cannot now figure the number of years from 1918 to 1995, but I know they have been many. Much has come and gone between then and now—even Jack.

One look at Jack's baby blanket and I remember it all.

Jack was born with a full head of thick, black hair. Where he got it from, I never knew. So many nights, I stood over his crib as he slept, running a hand through that hair. I rested my other hand on his little chest, which rose and fell in the shallow, uneven breaths of a sleeping baby. I ran my hands over those rows of blue and white and wondered what would become of us.

What will become of us?—I asked that same question as I traced my fingers around the white stars on the folded flag the uniformed men brought to the farmhouse a month before. John had been killed and buried somewhere in France on the second day of January. I remember that.

We named Jack after his father—John Franklin Carlson, Jr.

Carlson. That was their last name—Mom and Dad Carlson.

That was my last name too—my *second* last name. Charlotte Marie Carlson. John was my husband—my first husband—and the first to call me Lottie.

I always do this, intertwine my fingers in the stitches of red yarn. It stands out from the rows of blue and white. It reminds me of Jack.

In the summer of 1922, Dad Carlson took us on a touring vacation in his new car. His sons, John's younger brothers, were old enough by then to tend to the farm. So we packed the car and headed off to see Yellowstone National Park.

Jack had slept with that blanket every night of his first four years, even in the summer. One morning, as Dad cooked bacon over the campfire and Mom poured coffee (with grounds, I remember), little Jack stumbled out of the tent, dragging his blanket with him. It caught on a root and tore. Mom placed the coffee pot on the edge of the campfire. She sat on a stump, unraveled some yarn from the red potholder she had carried the coffee pot with, and she mended the blanket right on the spot.

By the time we got home, those red stitches were just as much a part of the blanket as the white and the blue. It was part of Jack's story. It was fitting—the red with the white and blue—a memory of Jack's father and that folded flag. Even more, it seemed to me, a picture of what Mom and Dad Carlson had been to me—to me and Jack—a stitch in the tear of our lives, holding us together, determined not to see us unravel.

It's never failed in all these years, as I've run my hands over this blanket, or even just caught sight of its red stitches, I remember Mom and Dad, and little Jack, and the blessing of a tear and a mend.

I almost—*almost*—parted with this blanket.

Mothers are meant to stand over cribs and run their hands through the thick black hair of their newborn sons. Mothers are meant to tuck blankets around their baby boys and whisper, "I love you. I will see you in the morning." A mother is not meant to stand over her son, asleep in a coffin, and say goodbye. But I have.

Oh, I'm not complaining. Well, I don't mean to. Jack had a good life, mostly. His death was not tragic, not like his father's.

Jack died in his sleep, in his own bed, in his own home in 1988, at the age of seventy. Really, what more could a mother want for her son than a long life and a peaceful death in his own bed? It's certainly better than dying as a teenaged boy, lying in a field of mud in the French countryside, hands over your bayonetted stomach, trying to hold your guts in, and calling for your wife as you bleed out, alone and scared. (At least, that's how I have imagined it all too vividly and, despite my prayers and best efforts, I cannot forget.)

Well, there *is* something more that a mother could want—to die first. A mother is not made to stand over the wrinkled face of her aged son, to brush his thinned gray hairs, to touch clammy hands folded over a breathless chest, and to tell him goodbye.

The doctor said that Jack died of "natural causes." But I was not fooled. I have lived enough to know that there is nothing "natural" about death. There is nothing natural about boys slaughtering boys over borders and boundaries. There is nothing natural about a seventy-year-old man turning out the lamp, pulling up the comforter, and never waking up. There is nothing natural about being ninety-five years old, being dressed by a young woman in pink pajamas, being unable to forget the things you never wanted to remember, and unable to remember the only things you ever wanted to keep. No, there is nothing natural about death or its causes—this too, I remember.

I almost put Jack's blanket in his casket. I had made it for him, after all. But I didn't. It wasn't just his blanket; it was *ours*. It wasn't his tear that Mom Carlson had stitched; it was *ours,* our life.

So I kept it, for me, so that I could remember those red stitches that mended my tear; so that I could remember those who mended me; so that I would remember to mend the tears I find; so that I could remember that there is a mend for every tear—even that cold, terrible, unnatural tear that has ripped my heart too often, and which will stop my own heart someday soon, I suppose.

Something wakes me. I must have dozed off again. There is a knock at the door.

"Come in," I try to call. My throat is dry and makes no sound, so I clear it to try again. "Come in."

The door opens, and the young woman in pink enters. *Sarah*, I remember.

"It's time for your medication, Lottie," she says, stopping at the kitchenette sink to fill a glass with water. She carries the glass in one hand and a small paper cup in the other.

I open a trembling hand to receive the pill and take the glass with the other. The pill goes down in one attempt today, and I am grateful.

"Thank you, Sarah."

She returns my smile. "You're looking a little better than you did earlier this morning, Lottie. Did you have a nap?"

"I believe so." I take another drink of water. It tastes good.

"Mid-morning is always a good time for you." Sarah smiles, taking the glass from me. "Are you ready for a cup of tea?"

"That would be wonderful. Thank you. Two

sugars and some cream. Please."

As Sarah prepares the tea, I look out the window at a squirrel. He is digging around the snowdrift at the bottom of the window and where there are open patches in the lawn. I'll bet he buried acorns here last fall, though he does not remember where. He contents himself with a random sunflower seed and moves on to dig another hole.

I remember now. This is my apartment. "Assisted living," they called it, though I seem to receive more assistance and do less living these days.

I remember that I do not remember. They told me that years ago. I have… I have… I do not remember what I have. I remember that I cannot remember.

But mid-morning is good. My memories rise and set with the sun, it seems. I know where I am now. And I know who is with me. That's always a good feeling.

"The same as usual, Lottie?" Sarah calls.

"Yes, thank you. The tea is in the cupboard above the sink."

Sarah unfolds a tray and places it in front of me, over my legs. "Do you mind if I join you?" she asks. "I have a break coming up."

"That would be nice."

"Oh good," she says, walking to the kitchenette. "I always enjoy our conversations. You're like the grandmother I never had." She arranges a small teapot, sugar, and creamer on a service tray. "There's a cup in the dish drainer, Lottie. Do you have another?"

"You can use this one here." I say, motioning to the cup that sits on the shelf next to me.

Sarah brings over the tea and service and begins to pour.

"Oh! There's a chip in this cup. Should I go find another?"

"No, no. This cup will do just fine."

Sarah prepares her tea and then returns the tea service to the kitchen.

I run my fingers around the rim of the old cup, flat and broad, with a finger hole in the handle large enough for two of my fingers. It is the color of fresh cream with a thin stripe of blue near the top. I lift it with both hands to sip the tea, still too hot, and set it down. I finger the chip in the rim of the cup.

"A chipped cup can still serve tea," I say,

not looking up.

"I'm sorry?" Sarah replies, sitting down to her tea.

"My mother used to say that—'A chipped cup can still serve tea.' This was my father's cup. That's why it's so big; it fit his hand. He was a large man."

I try another sip and then set the cup down to cool.

"My father drank his coffee from this mug. My mother was the tea drinker. Every morning at a half-past nine and every afternoon at a quarter of three, my mother would brew the coffee on our kitchen stove—a wood-burning stove in those days. I would get my father's cup down and put in two spoonfuls of sugar. We would have it ready—hot and sweet—when father came in."

"Awww." Sarah sighs. "How nice!"

Not looking up, I continue, "One day, we were late getting the coffee on and were rushing to have it ready when father came in. In my haste, I bumped the cup against the shelf and chipped it."

"Father was so angry. 'Do you know what this cup cost?!' he shouted. 'Now it's good for nothing!' I was so scared. In those days, when mother took us into town, she might give us each a penny to spend on candy—and that was a treat! How would I ever buy a new cup?"

"So, what happened?" Sarah asks between sips.

"My mother took another cup down from the cupboard, poured his coffee, and served him. Then, she set his chipped cup down at her place and filled it with tea. She lifted it (just like this) and took a sip. Then she set it down and looked at me and said, 'Charlotte, a chipped cup can still serve tea. Don't you ever forget that.'"

"And, you know?" I say, lifting the cup. "I never did."

"Awww." Sarah tilts her head, giving me that look of exaggerated pity and affirmation that the young give to the old, thinking we don't notice. But we do. "It sounds like you really loved your mom and dad."

"Yes, I loved my mother. She was a saint." I lean forward, raise my cup, and sip my tea. I set it down and finger the chip again. "My father was a mean bastard."

Sarah laughs, uncomfortable, startled at an old woman's vulgarity.

I lean back in my chair, close my eyes, and breathe.

My father was a mean bastard. I mean that literally.

He was a bastard. In those days, people still used that word of a child born to unwed parents. It was easier to say than "illegitimate child," and it did a more thorough job of driving home the status of illegitimacy, both to the community and to the child.

I do not know much about my father's childhood or his parents. I know that my grandfather never married my grandmother. I know that he never knew my father.

I know that my grandmother's surname was O'Connor. (That was my last name—my *first* last name—and my father's only last name.) I know that she raised my father until he was ten years old. I know nothing of her after that.

I know that my father went to live in an orphanage at the age of ten. I know that he ran away when he turned fourteen.

And I know that my father was mean.

I was seven years old when my eye was injured. It was my first year to attend school in the one-room country school.

I am the youngest of four children. I have — or had—three older brothers. (They are all gone now.) Frank, the oldest, was six years older than me; I believe it was his last year to attend school. George was four years older than me. Leonard, my closest playmate, was two years older. They were good brothers who grew up to be good men.

It was October, I think. The leaves had turned. I had dilly-dallied in the schoolyard, as little girls are prone to do, jumping off the front steps of the schoolhouse and filling my lunch pail with acorns to feed to our hogs. My brothers knew better than to arrive home late; father expected the chores to be done by dinner. So, they had gone ahead without me.

When I arrived at our farm, I knew immediately that something was wrong. There was a tub of laundry on the front lawn. Next to it lay a wet bedsheet. Mother never let her bedsheets so much as brush the grass. But, here one lay, sopping wet, right there on the ground.

I scanned the barnyard. Three sets of schoolbooks, each still cinched in a belt, lie in the grass between the house and the corncrib. I walked to them. As I stooped to pick them up, I heard shouting from the far side of the corncrib.

I ran to it and entered through the small door in the southern bin. I hoped to view the commotion from a place of safety. Looking up, through the slats in the siding, I saw the silhouettes of my mother and my brothers outside. They were lined up in a row against the side of the corncrib. I ran to the wall and peeked through.

"Where the hell is the rest of my whiskey?" My father, obviously drunk, paced before the lineup. "I swear to God I'll put a bullet through the heads of every goddam one a' ya!" He pointed his rifle at each one in turn. Then, he turned and walked out into the yard toward the field, hollering at no one and everyone at once. He stooped and picked up an empty whiskey bottle.

"Momma," I whispered through the slats. "Momma, I'm scared."

Startled at the sound of my voice, my mother turned her head and whispered, "Charlotte! Go to the house, Charlotte. Go and hide, baby. Go and hide now!"

"Damn it, woman!" my father screamed. "I told you to keep quiet!" He hurled the empty bottle at my mother. It struck the side of the corncrib, right where I was peeking through the slats, and shattered. A shard of glass hit my left eye. It felt like someone had pressed a red-hot needle right into my pupil.

I screamed in pain and fell to the ground. Mother was howling my name. The next thing I knew, she was holding me on the corncrib floor and screaming at my father and trying to look at my injured eye by the dusty light that streamed in through the siding.

I did not see what happened next outside the corncrib. But, I heard the story many times over the years.

The sound of my scream stunned my father. As he stood there confused and trying to understand what had happened, Frank ran toward him, driving a shoulder into his gut, and taking him to the ground. There was no way that Frank could lick our father. He knew that. That wasn't why he tackled him, not because he thought he would win.

My father dropped the rifle when he fell to the ground. George scooped it up and ran away with it, while Frank and my father struggled on the ground. George hid the rifle—and he hid it good too. It wasn't the first time our father ever lined his family up against the corncrib and aimed his gun at them, but it was the last.

Though I didn't see this particular beating, I could see it in my mind, because I had seen it too many times before. My father would have a grip on Frank's wrist, and Frank would be flailing desperately, trying to escape, while father undid his belt with his other hand and removed it.

Forty-eight inches of thick leather. As my mother carried me to the house, I could hear it pop and snap through each belt loop. We had a woodshed, and my father dragged Frank behind it.

I sat on a stool in the corner of the kitchen, holding a warm, wet cloth to my eye. George and

Leonard stood near me. We all jumped when the kitchen door flew open. My father dragged Frank through the door and dropped him on the floor, dropped him like a wet bed sheet for mother to deal with. He had whipped Frank with that belt until his shirt had torn to shreds.

Have you ever seen a man whipped until his shirt fell off? I have. *No*—I have seen a *boy*, a *thirteen-year-old boy*, whipped until his shirt was rags. This, too, I remember. I didn't know if Frank was alive, and if he was alive, I didn't know if he would live.

My mother did not say a word. She knew better. She filled a bowl with water and set to cleaning out his cuts, right there on the kitchen floor.

My father turned toward us and said,

"George, where is my rifle?"

My brother stood there—straight and tall and unflinching and eleven years old—and looked silently up at our father. I have never seen such courage in all my life.

"Tell me where my rifle is, George."

George said, "No, sir."

My father took my brother by the wrist and turned and led him out the door. George did not fight him or make a noise—he walked, silent and willing, to pay the price it cost to protect our family.

I don't know how long George was with our father, but when his whipping was over, my father brought him back into the kitchen. George did not receive the same whipping Frank had. Father was growing tired and sober.

George's lips pinched together in a thin line. His stoic face showed the tracks of drying tears. He walked to Frank, bent over with a faint grimace, and picked up the bowl of bloody water that sat next to our kneeling mother. He dumped it in the yard, filled it at the pump, and returned with fresh water.

My father turned toward Leonard and me. He said, "Leonard, tell Papa where the rifle is."

Leonard only shook his head and trembled.

My father stepped toward him, extended a hand, and said, "Come with Papa then, Leonard."

I do not know who my mother surprised more—Leonard and me, our father, or herself— but she charged into the pantry and returned with a large metal canister that read FLOUR. She removed the lid and turned the canister upside down.

The flour slid out of it, holding the shape of the cylinder until it hit the floor and exploded, filling the kitchen with a cloud of white dust. My mother knelt in the middle of it all, her fingers sifting through the small pile of flour that remained.

She rose, looking like a ghost, her arms and fingers pink with the dough of flour and blood. She took my father's hand, turned it palm up, and looked him in the eye.

"Here," she said, pressing into his hand a small collection of flour-dusted coins and dollar bills—currency that she had earned or found and hidden and saved. "Go and buy a rifle or more of your damn whiskey. But when this is gone, that's all there is. And don't you *ever* lay a finger on one of our children again."

He never did lay a finger on any of us again. Frank lived—and he grew up to be a good man.

I had good brothers. They all grew up to be such good men.

My eye did not heal properly. A scar developed, right over the pupil, giving it a cloudy appearance. That's why it can only see shapes and colors.

Despite it all, my mother stayed with our father until the end. *Why did she stay? Would I have stayed?* That, I do not know.

In those days, where we were, there were not many options for a woman in my mother's situation. To leave my father, to go and take four children with her, would have been to resign us all to destitution. She would not have been able to remarry. She would not have been able to earn enough to support us. The work required simply to get by would have left her with no time to be a mother to us. She was set on raising us children, on loving us. And, I believe, she really did love our father somehow.

My mother often said that all a man has in this world—the only thing he's born with, and the only thing he can take to the grave—is the dignity of being a human being. That is how she treated our father—with the dignity of being human. Even when she had to intervene to protect her children—for we too, she insisted, were human beings—she treated him as a man and not a monster. And when my father was dying from a pickled liver, my mother nursed him and loved him and buried him with dignity.

Anyway, my father was a mean bastard.

I'm awakened by the sound of clinking cups. Someone is washing dishes. Sarah smiles at me. "You fell asleep, Lottie. Do you need anything before I go?" she asks, walking over and standing near me.

I offer my hand, which she takes with her left, which is soft and warm and smooth— *young*. She wears no ring.

"Sarah," I say, reaching and resting my other hand on her round stomach. I am old and do not see well, but there are things you cannot hide from a woman who has lived these many years. I wait for her to look at me. "Sarah, a chipped cup can still serve tea. Don't you ever forget that."

"Oh, I won't, Lottie. I won't." She quickly turns and goes.

I'm jarred awake by the sound of a bird flying into the window. They do that sometimes, especially at this time of day. The sparrow does not seem to be hurt, only regretting its haste in leaving the feeder.

The clock reads a quarter to twelve, and the sun is shining through the window onto my legs and lap. I remember where I am. I am content.

There is a knock at the door. It opens before I can answer.

"Good morning, Mrs. Barnes," says a young woman in pink pajamas. "Just checking if you'll be joining us for lunch today."

As she approaches, I see that this is a different young woman in pink.

"Where is Sarah?"

"Sarah's shift ends at noon. But I think she's back at midnight. I'm sure she'll check on you."

I try to look up at her. I raise my hand to block the glare of the sun, which is reflecting off the glass sides of the bird feeder. A blue jay is on the feeder now, scattering seed on the snowdrift below as he searches for sunflower seeds. I do not like that blue jay. I wish the sparrows would return.

"Is that sun too bright?" she asks, walking toward the edge of the window. Before I can reply, she begins lowering the blinds. I do not want them shut. I want to feel the sun and see the sparrows. She closes them anyway.

"So would you like to join us in the dining hall?"

"No," I mutter, folding my hands in my lap and looking at the closed blinds. "But thank you."

"Sarah said you haven't been eating much this week. Are you feeling okay?"

I take a breath to answer and open my mouth, but I only smile and nod.

"Can I bring you something? Maybe some soup and crackers?"

I smile and nod again, and she leaves.

I have no interest in returning to the dining hall—and not only because I have no appetite. That man is there. I do not remember his name, but I remember him.

That man likes to sit with the women. We are

mostly women here. There are few men. The ladies seem to enjoy his attention, though I do not.

Some time ago, I was sitting in front of the aviary at the end of our hallway. I like to go there to rest and to listen to the birds sing. That afternoon, I was resting in a chair with my eyes closed, listening to a finch.

"Hello, Charlotte."

I opened my eyes.

"Hello."

"Enjoying the birds?"

"Yes, and resting my eyes a spell."

"Don't mind me," he said. He began to whistle, imitating the finch.

I rested my head against the chair and closed my eyes again.

His whistling stopped.

Then—to my surprise—he kissed me on the mouth.

As of that day, it had been almost thirty-seven years since a man had kissed me on the mouth.

I had never kissed a man (or a boy, for that matter) until the day John Franklin Carlson asked me to marry him. I was seventeen years old.

John and I had known each other for years. His family lived across the section, and we attended the same one-room country school. He was a year ahead of me.

When we were old enough—he was seventeen, and I was sixteen—he would escort me to the dances held on the first Friday of each month up in Eden, at the City Hall.

When I asked my mother if I could go with

John to that first dance, she didn't say yes or no. She only said, "You'll never find a more selfless man than a Carlson." And, to this day, I have not.

It was April 6, 1917—a cool Friday evening. The talk at the dance that night had been of the Great War that was going on over in Europe, and the Selective Service Act that had just been approved in Washington, D.C.

John was especially quiet—unusually serious—as he drove me home in his father's cart. "Did you hear the talk of the War, Lottie?"

"Yes. I did."

"They're saying America will enter, but we need more soldiers."

I did not answer him. I only looked out over the horses pulling us along in the moonlight.

"I'm going to enlist."

Neither of us spoke for the rest of the ride.

As he turned the horses up our drive, I began to cry. John reached over and took my hand. I tensed a bit and almost pulled away. He'd never touched me before without asking.

"Lottie," he said softly, bringing the team to a halt. He waited for my reply.

I cleared my throat, wiping the tears from my cheeks. I turned to him. The moon was almost full, and he looked simply beautiful in its light. "Yes, John?"

"Lottie." It was the only time I can ever recall seeing him nervous. He looked down at our hands, then into my eyes. "Lottie, if your father will give his blessing, would you marry me?"

I simply nodded. I couldn't speak for the joy and the fear that filled me.

John climbed down from the cart, leaving me sitting there in the moonlight. He walked to the house and knocked on the door. I heard the surprise in my father's voice when he opened the door and welcomed him in.

After a few minutes, John emerged from the house and returned to the wagon. He helped me down, took my hands, and knelt on one knee, right there in the grass. He looked up at me and said, "Charlotte O'Connor, will you marry me?"

This time, I was ready to speak. "Yes, John. I would be honored."

He stood and took my face in his hands and kissed me on the mouth—my very first kiss—beneath the full moon in my father and mother's front yard.

We were married four weeks later in the

front room of the Carlson home. Reverend Ellis, the Carlsons' minister, officiated. Our family didn't have a minister.

When June arrived, John was off to be trained as a soldier. I was, unbeknownst to any of us, pregnant with our son—a son who would be fatherless the day he was born.

Most of the young men my age had gone to fight in the war. Of those who returned, most of them had either married before they left or were returning to a waiting sweetheart. If there were any eligible bachelors, none showed the slightest interest in a widow with an orphaned son.

I had no gentleman callers (and certainly no gentleman kissers) for a full ten years after John's death. I had all but given up hope of remarrying and had become content—satisfied, really—with devoting my attention to raising Jack and helping Mom and Dad Carlson on the farm.

Then came Christmas Eve, 1928. We drove into town for the candlelight service at the Eden Presbyterian Church. As we were leaving, I slipped on a bit of ice on the stairs and fell. I must have struck my head quite hard, because the next thing I knew, I was lying on my back on a church pew, surrounded by a crowd of people who were looking down at me and whispering to one another. There, kneeling at my side, was a man that I had never seen. He was asking me if my head hurt and what year it was and who was president and whether I knew where I was. I couldn't answer a single one of those questions either—not because I had hit my head, but because half the county, it seemed, was staring down at me and whispering. And there is nothing I hate more than being the center of attention. I simply couldn't think!

Well, eventually, I sat up, and I called Jack to come sit with me. The poor boy was scared to death by it all.

Satisfied that I was fine, the congregation finally went home. But this man, the one who had been asking all the questions, insisted on helping me out to the Carlsons' car. When we got to the farm, and Dad opened the car door for me, this man was there to help me out of the car. (He had followed us back to the farm!) He helped me to the house.

That man, as I was soon to discover, was Dr. Everett Barnes.

"Thank you, Everett," Mom said as she took my arm to help me to my room.

"It's my pleasure, Mrs. Carlson. You keep watch on her and send for me first thing if you have any concerns."

"I will," Mom replied. "Tell your aunt 'Merry Christmas' from me. And have a Merry Christmas yourself, Everett. It's so good to see you again."

"I will, Mrs. Carlson. A Merry Christmas to you both, Mr. and Mrs. Carlson."

Then he turned to Jack. "I don't believe I've met you, young man. My apologies." He leaned toward him and extended a hand. "I am Everett Barnes."

Jack shook his hand. "I'm Jack." He cleared his throat and said again, "I am John, John Carlson."

Mr. Barnes looked at Dad. "He's the spitting image of his father. Doesn't seem so long ago that we were putting up hay, and there was a John Carlson about his size trying to lend a hand." He looked from Mom to Dad and back to Mom. "I wish he was here now. I'm so sorry."

Then he smiled suddenly and looked at Jack. "It's a pleasure to meet you, Jack. You all have a very Merry Christmas."

"Merry Christmas to you too, *Doctor* Barnes," Dad said with a laugh and closed the door behind the departing guest.

The next day, just as we were finishing our Christmas dinner, there was a knock at the door. It was Dr. Everett Barnes. He had come to check on me.

"Come in, come in!" Mom said. "We were

just about to have pie and coffee. Can you stay?"

So Dr. Everett Barnes sat at our dining room table and drank coffee and ate pie and exchanged stories with Mom and Dad Carlson. I learned through those stories that he was the nephew of a widow who lived in town. While his uncle was alive, he spent his summers at their place. Since his aunt and uncle were friends of the Carlsons, he knew them and knew John and worked the summers at the Carlson farm, helping Dad.

As I began to clear the dishes, he insisted on helping me. He stood in the kitchen, drying the dishes as I washed them, engaging me in the most natural conversation I had ever enjoyed in my life.

When we finished, Mom and Dad were

asleep in their chairs in the living room, and Jack was occupied with his new toy. Everett asked if I would like to go for a walk.

It was a warm and sunny day for December, and we walked for almost two hours. We walked the roads around our section, and I showed him where the farm had been where I grew up. My father had died a year after Jack's birth and my mother a year later. My brothers divided the land, tore down the buildings, plowed the acreage under, and carried off every last reminder of the place.

I learned that Everett was a widower. After school, he moved to a small town outside of Indianapolis and set up a family practice—and also a family. He married a girl named Katie. After ten years of marriage, Katie died giving birth, and the baby girl died too.

Everett remained where he was, mostly, he said, because he had nowhere else to go. He never remarried, he said, because there wasn't anyone to marry in that little town. He was now forty-four years old. He was back in town for a few weeks around the holidays to check in on his aunt, the only living family that he had.

He stopped at the farm every afternoon that week—to check on how I was coming along after my fall, is what he said—and we took long walks. (That was something we would always do. That man just loved to walk.)

That Sunday, December 30, at Mom's insistence, he joined us after church for dinner. After we had finished eating, Jack went out to play in the afternoon sun. Mom served us coffee and gooseberry pie for dessert. Just as I was about to take a bite of my pie, Everett said, as naturally as if he was asking for someone to pass the sugar, "Mr. and Mrs. Carlson, I wonder if I might have Charlotte's hand in marriage."

Imagine my surprise! A week earlier, I had not known this man from Adam. And now, here he was asking my in-laws if he could ask me to marry him.

Mom Carlson simply smiled, as though she knew this was coming, and she looked from me to Dad and back to Everett. Dad cleared his throat and set down his fork. "Well, Lottie's a grown woman, Everett. She can make that decision for herself. But I will say this: We love Lottie. And we love that young Jack. They're the only things we have left in this world to love and remind us of John. Nothing would delight us more than to know that you will love her and care for her — *and* that you will love and be a father to our grandson. And I know you would."

Then Everett turned to me and said, "Charlotte, would you be my wife?"

"Yes," I heard myself say. "I would like that very much."

We were married the next Sunday, January 6, 1929, in a small ceremony at the church in Eden. Reverend Ellis officiated, with Mom and Dad Carlson serving as witnesses and Jack as Everett's best man. I wore the ring that John had given me, and

Everett wore the ring that Katie had given him. They were perfectly good rings, and our spouses had been a part of our lives—a *good* part of our lives—and why should they be discarded and forgotten now, simply because they had died?

That day, Everett Barnes became the second man to kiss me, and I became Mrs. Barnes. My third last name—my *last* last name.

A week after the wedding, Everett returned to Indiana and made arrangements to sell his practice to a young graduate from the university. Then he returned to stay with me and with Jack and with Mom and Dad Carlson.

Everett bought the farm from the Carlsons. They lived with us there in the farmhouse until they passed away. Then we lived there, the three of us, until Jack went off to college. And then we lived there, just the two of us — except for the summers—and we enjoyed our walks and ourselves.

We had a good marriage, a delightful marriage, really. I loved Everett, and he loved me. Everett loved Jack like his own son. And Jack loved him. And we were happy.

Everett was forty-four when we married; I was a month shy of twenty-nine. I believe that is why our marriage worked: he was young enough to marry an old woman like me.

There is an oldness—and not a good oldness—that settles on a person, even a young person, when they have walked through seasons of grief and disappointment. There is a seriousness that settles on a person when they have felt the weight of loss and responsibility and worry. I felt that weight with John's death, and I still felt that weight thinking of Jack's future. I had become an old woman at the age of twenty-eight.

But there is also a youth that returns as one grows older. After you've lived long enough in this broken-down old world, and seen the vanity of striving after the wind and felt the sting of the thorn and the thistle, you learn that, as the Preacher says, "There is nothing better for a man, than that he should eat and drink, and that he should make his soul enjoy good in his labour." That is what Everett had become—a young man again, a man who knew how to eat and drink and enjoy good. Everett had aged well through his losses, and passed through old age, and regained a youthfulness that only seemed to grow.

So he was young enough to marry an old woman like me. That is why our marriage worked: he could lead me through what another, *younger* man could not. And, I think, he helped me to become young again, even in my old age.

Everett had a stroke in the summer of 1958. He slipped into a coma, and the doctor told us that he would not live. So I stood at his bedside, and thanked him for all that he had been to me, and held his hand, and kissed him, and said goodbye.

Everett was seventy-four years old when he died; I was fifty-eight.

That was the last time anyone ever kissed me.

Only two men had ever kissed me, two men that I loved and who loved me. Now that man—that nameless man—has kissed me. And he will be the last man to ever kiss me. That makes me sad now. I wish it could be undone, but it cannot.

"Mrs. Barnes? Mrs. Barnes, are you okay?" A young woman dressed in pink is kneeling beside my chair and rubbing my hands.

"Where am I? Who are you?"

Fear fills my chest.

She looks concerned. "I think you were having a bad dream. Are you okay, Mrs. Barnes? You're trembling." She asks me if I want the soup she brought.

"No. I'm not hungry."

The light in the room is strange, glowing

from behind the lowered blinds. I do not know where I am. I do not know who the young woman in pink is.

She brings me a glass of water. I take a drink and breathe.

"Would you like the blinds open?"

I nod.

She opens the blinds.

A blue jay outside my window is picking the sunflower seeds from the bird feeder, scattering the rest of the seed on the ground below. I do not like the blue jay. I wish he would fly away. I wish the sparrows would come back, but they will not.

I have been asleep in my chair. The room is dim, unlit. The window blinds are open, and the pastel light of a setting sun that I cannot see reflects off the snow outside my window. It fills the room with a faint glow.

It will be dinnertime soon, and I have not prepared anything for dinner, and Everett will be coming in from the barn soon. I am agitated, angry at my own laziness.

"Lottie, you fool, sleeping the afternoon away!" I scold myself. The sound of my voice startles me. I do not recognize it. It sounds so...so old.

I must get up and cook dinner for Everett and Jack. They will be in soon.

Why am I draped in Jack's baby blanket? This is not my chair.

This doesn't make sense, any of it. I never sleep in a chair in the afternoon. Jack's blanket should be on his bed.

Anyhow, I must get up and cook dinner for Everett and Jack. They will be in soon.

There is a knock at the door. It takes me a moment to understand what I am hearing. *Who could that be?*

I try to rise to answer the door, but I cannot. I am not strong enough.

The knocking continues.

"Come in," says the old woman whose voice I now recognize as my own. Perhaps I have been ill, and that is why my voice sounds strange, and I have Jack's blanket, and I cannot lift myself out of this chair.

The door opens a crack, letting a shaft of light fall through and across the floor. The silhouette of a man fills the doorway.

"Hello?" I call.

"Mrs. Barnes? May I come in? It's Pastor."

Ah! Reverend Ellis. I must be ill, and he is coming to call on me. He is always so kind like that.

"Come in," I reply.

"May I turn on the light, Mrs. Barnes?"

Before I can answer, I hear the switch flip as a sudden, stark brightness fills the room. My eyes shut and water as I strain to open them.

"It's good to see you, Mrs. Barnes," Reverend Ellis says. Only, it does not sound like Reverend Ellis. He seems younger, much younger. "I'm sorry I'm a bit late today. I won't stay long; I know you have dinner soon."

"Oh! You'll have to excuse me, Reverend Ellis," I say, trying to push myself up from my chair. "I need to go make dinner. Everett and Jack will be in soon."

"Everett? Jack?" Reverend Ellis sounds confused.

I look up and force my eyes to open to look at my guest. A young man sits in the chair across from me. He is not Reverend Ellis. I do not recognize him at all. I do not know this room either.

"Who are you? Where am I?" I am growing agitated. I feel angry and afraid. "Where is Everett?"

"I'm Pastor Thompson, from the church."

"Where is Reverend Ellis?"

"Mrs. Barnes," he says, shifting in his seat.

"Who are you?"

"I'm Pastor Thompson, from the church. I've been there for eight years now. I visit in the afternoon and read you the Bible, and we pray. Remember?"

I do not remember.

"Where is Everett?"

He does not reply but looks down at the book in his hands.

"Where is Everett!?" I demand. I am angry now.

The man I do not know looks up at me. "Mrs. Barnes, Everett isn't here anymore."

"Where did he go?"

He does not reply. Instead, he opens the book in his hands. "Would it be okay if I read a bit, Mrs. Barnes?"

"Who are you?" I do not know who he is or why he is here. I want to see Everett.

"I'm Pastor Thompson, Mrs. Barnes." He holds up the open book. "Would it be okay if I read from the Gospel of John, Mrs. Barnes?"

"Where is Revered Ellis? I would very much like to see Reverend Ellis."

"We're at chapter one this afternoon, Mrs. Barnes."

"Are you Reverend Ellis?" I ask. He does not look like Reverend Ellis.

"Yes, ma'am." Reverend Ellis smiles. I see now that he has had his hair cut and is wearing a new shirt, and so perhaps he looks younger. Perhaps that is why I do not recognize him.

"Where is Everett? I want to see him."

He reaches over and takes my hand. "Everett is gone now, Mrs. Barnes. But you'll see him soon."

At his assurance and exhausted from my confusion, I recline in my chair and close my eyes, trying to relax until Everett returns.

"John, chapter one," Reverend Ellis says, and then begins to read. "In the beginning was the Word, and the Word was with God, and the Word was God…"

I like the sound of Reverend Ellis' voice, reading the Bible; it makes me think of sitting in the church with Mom and Dad Carlson, and later with Everett, and hearing the Scripture readings and the sermons. I was not raised in the church, though I saw my mother read her Bible. So attending the Sunday services was a new experience for me after I married John. I did not know anything of the Bible, and so I listened to every word Reverend Ellis read.

He is reading now, in his gentle voice, "And the Word was made flesh, and dwelt among us, (and we beheld his glory, the glory as of the only begotten of the Father,) full of grace and truth."

The voice of Reverend Ellis is a sound of comfort to me. His voice pronounced John and me to be "man and wife." His voice spoke words of assurance at John's funeral service. John's body stayed in France, but Reverend Ellis officiated a service so that we could remember and mourn.

The whole town turned out that day. I sat in the front pew next to Dad, who sat next to Mom. Dad had an arm around each of us. I remember that I kept my hands on my stomach, cradling the one piece of John that I still could.

The baby was especially still through the whole service, which was unusual. I was afraid I had lost both my baby and my husband. But then, he moved a little. I thought perhaps he knew where we were and what was happening. I thought maybe he was still out of respect for his father. I remember thinking that perhaps he was sad, too, with my sadness. You never can tell what they know in the womb. It wouldn't surprise me. Jack was a *good* boy—and he grew up to be a *good* man too, despite it all.

Reverend Ellis preached a message from Second Corinthians, a passage that I would commit to memory: *"But we have this treasure in earthen vessels, that the excellency of the power may be of God, and not of us. ...For we which live are alway delivered unto death for Jesus' sake, that the life also of Jesus might be made manifest in our mortal flesh."*

Reverend Ellis said that John's death was a "manifestation" of the life of Jesus. That seemed a strange thing to me at the time. But over the years, as I dwelt on that word and on that verse and on John's death, I began to understand what he might have meant. There was a great evil at work in Europe, and John had volunteered to go fight it, and he had died so that people could be free from it—a "manifestation" of Jesus. That thought would give meaning to John's death, and therefore to my loss. And that gave me comfort.

And Reverend Ellis' voice comforts me now, as he reads, "Behold the Lamb of God, which taketh away the sin of the world."

Reverend Ellis baptized Jack and me on the same Sunday morning. It was a Sunday in March—a bright Sunday morning; I remember shafts of stained-glass light landing on Jack's face, and I thought it was beautiful and wished that John could be there to see his boy.

Mom and Dad Carlson stood beside me at the front of the church, next to the baptismal font. I had Jack wrapped in his blanket of blue and white.

Revered Ellis dipped the cloth into the water and turned to me. He wiped the wet cloth across my forehead and said, "In the name of the Father, and of the Son, and of the Holy Ghost. Amen."

Then, I handed Jack to Reverend Ellis, who held him in one arm over the baptismal font. He scooped three handfuls of water over Jack's forehead and said, "In the name of the Father, and of the Son, and of the Holy Ghost. Amen." Jack cried a little, and I laughed a bit because I thought it was lovely. Reverend Ellis took a white linen cloth and wiped Jack's forehead and handed him back to me. And Jack was comforted.

Then he placed a hand on my forehead and his other hand on Jack's head, and he said, "Therefore we are buried with him by baptism into death: that like as Christ was raised up from the dead by the glory of the Father, even so we also should walk in newness of life."

You know—this will sound silly, I am sure—but I felt as though that morning that Reverend Ellis was the first man to give me a kiss. He did not kiss me, not like John and Everett (and now that man) kissed me. They *kissed* me. But Reverend Ellis *gave* me a kiss. It felt as though I had been kissed on the forehead, right there in the front of the church. As I thought about it, I knew that I had been. It was as though, through Reverend Ellis' hand and the water and the words that he spoke, God himself had bent down and kissed me on the forehead and said, "You are my daughter now, and Jack is my son, and I will care for you as my own, and I will never leave you nor forsake you, even to the end of the age." And in that moment, I trusted him—I trusted God—as though he was my own husband, and I was comforted.

That's what I thought—and that's what I still think—and it comforts me, even to this day.

I wake to the sound of music. The blinds are closed. A lamp is on, and I am in my bed. I cannot remember anyone helping me to bed. But here I am.

A television is on. A man's voice announces, "Ladies and gentlemen, it's the Lawrence Welk Show!" Lawrence Welk appears with his baton and introduces a group of square dancers in front of a barn door, dancing to the "Orange Blossom Special."

"Let's have a barn dance!" Everett said one evening. "For our kids!"

Our kids. That's what we called them. Everett and I wouldn't have any children of our own, at least not in the conventional manner. But we had kids—a hundred of them, I would guess!

The very first summer after Everett bought the farm from Mom and Dad Carlson, he hired a young man to help him. The boy was sixteen years old, the son of an old friend of Everett's in

Indiana. He had been in some trouble back home, and Everett offered to let him work on our farm for the summer "to get away from it all for a spell," as Everett would say.

I didn't know it at first—though I learned the story, bit by bit—but this was more or less how Everett had come to stay with his aunt and work with Mom and Dad Carlson in his youth. He was getting away from it all for a spell. "Don't know where I'd be now," he said at Dad Carlson's funeral, "if it hadn't been for a gracious old man who taught me how to work and how to live."

Naturally, at first, I was a bit concerned about the influence a troubled young man might have on Jack. But, you know, Jack looked up to him like a big brother, the same way he looked up to

Everett as a father. He followed them around just about everywhere, doing what they did, learning what that young man learned. That young man seemed to take Jack under his wing, the same way Everett did with him.

The next two summers, that young man came back again. The year Jack turned twelve, Everett hired two more kids from town, the same age as Jack. He taught those boys how to work hard and take responsibility and be gentlemen.

Every year, Everett would bring back the boys who wanted to work for him, and he would hire two more twelve-year-olds. Some of those boys would work the summer on our farm from the age of twelve until they were twenty-one, coming back from college over the summer to work and to help teach the younger boys.

After enough years, we might have upwards of twenty young men working for us. Most of the younger ones lived in Eden and came out every morning. Those from out of town stayed in our guest room or in the makeshift bunks that Everett eventually built out in the barn.

Everett worked those young men hard— from sunup to sundown. They would do everything, from walking the beans to putting up hay to tending our animals to painting the house and barn. The older boys would be given responsibility for crews of younger ones and would teach the younger ones all the things Everett had been teaching them.

It was an amazing thing to watch, really. It was as though Everett had started a summer school for turning boys into men. It even got so that parents were asking Everett a year in advance if their kids could come work on the farm—sometimes offering to let them work for free! Everett even bought my mother and father's old farmland from my brothers as they retired—not because we needed more land, but because those boys needed land to work.

As you can imagine, the feeding of twenty young farmhands was no small task. I was kept busy from before sunup to after sundown just fixing their breakfast, lunch, and dinner and cleaning up. As I watched Everett those first few years and began to understand what he was doing (and to understand where this was going!), an idea struck me. I asked Everett what he might think if I hired a few young girls from town to come out each day to help me with the cooking and cleaning and such. Everett thought it was a wonderful idea. So I did it.

I followed Everett's example. Each summer, I brought out a couple of young girls and invited them back the next, if they desired. Soon we had almost as many young women working for us as we had young men.

One summer, when Jack was eighteen, we counted thirty-seven young men and women sitting in our backyard, eating dinner and singing songs, and pitching horseshoes among the fireflies. As we watched them, Everett turned to me and said, "Let's have a barn dance—for our kids!"

So we did. Every Saturday night that summer, and each summer after, from June through August, we had a barn dance. The kids—*our kids*—would make all the preparations each Saturday after the work was done. A local band or square dance caller would come out. The kids would dance and dance late into the evening.

Everett's only stipulation was that those who went to the dance had to be up for church on Sunday morning. And, you know—they were! Reverend Ellis would shake his head in amazement at the pews full of young people, present and attentive each Lord's Day.

Everett loved those kids. And they loved him. They would have done anything for that man. And he for them, I know.

They were good boys and good girls. And they grew up to be good men and good women.

Everett brought out that first young man

in the summer of 1929. We did this every summer until 1954, the year Everett turned seventy and decided we would move to town. Twenty-five years of raising children. We must have had a hundred kids.

When Everett passed in 1958, you would not believe the number of those men and women who returned for the funeral. The church was standing-room-only, packed with the faces of those I fed as scrawny twelve-year-olds—now all grown-up. Some were married; some were even holding their own little children. One by one, as Jack and I greeted them, so many would say to us, "I don't know where I'd be if it hadn't been for Mr. Barnes."

A knock at the door wakes me. The room is dark.

I am in bed and try to get out, but I do not have the strength. The bed is inclined, so I can see the line of light that slips in beneath the door and spreads across the floor.

"Come in," I whisper so softly that I cannot hear myself.

The door opens. The light is bright, and I shut my eyes. I raise a hand to block some of the light until my eyes adjust.

I can make out the silhouette of a man, standing there and looking in. But I do not recognize him, even when I close my bad eye. I cannot see his face.

"*John*?" I whisper. "What are you doing up, dear? Do you need something?"

Then I see the hand I am holding up in front of my face, wrinkled and spotted and old. I fold my hands in my lap, and I feel Jack's baby blanket, and, by habit, my fingers go to the stitches of red yarn, and I remember the tear. I remember that John is dead and that he died long ago.

I cannot remember where I am or why I am here. I feel myself growing confused and agitated and afraid.

"Everett?" I say. But the man does not move. "Who are you?"

The man extends his hand and speaks my name. No, he does not call me Charlotte or Lottie. He does not call me Miss O'Connor or Mrs. John Carlson, or even Mrs. Barnes. He calls me by *my name*—a name that I did not even know that I had, that I have never heard before, though I know it at once. It is my name, my *real* name, my *last* name.

"Oh." I laugh, and I smile. "It's *you*."

I sit up and rise from the bed, as easily as I did as a six-year-old girl, jumping off the steps of the one-room schoolhouse. I begin to walk toward him.

Someone else appears in the doorway. It is a young woman dressed in pink. I know her. It is Sarah.

Sarah reaches her hand along the wall, searching for the light switch, and turns on the light. She looks toward me, and there is alarm and then sadness on her face. "Mrs. Barnes?" Sarah does not look at me. She looks through me, past me. I turn, following her gaze, to the bed.

Now I see what she sees. There is my

body, like a Sunday dress laid out in the evening after I have worn it and am preparing to put it away. My hands are folded on my lap, a finger intertwined in the red stitches in Jack's blanket.

As I look, I remember—I remember *everything*. And I am filled with deep thankfulness. I am thankful for that old blanket, and even for the tear—for, without it, there would be no mend.

Sarah passes me and walks to the bedside. She is stroking the old woman's hair and crying and smiling and saying, "Oh, Lottie. I'll miss you."

I turn away from her now, toward the door again, toward him. I am no longer afraid.

I take his hand and follow him home.

Eric Schumacher is an author, songwriter, and pastor who lives with his family in Iowa. Learn more at emschumacher.com.

CPSIA information can be obtained
at www.ICGtesting.com
Printed in the USA
LVHW091342070821
694453LV00007B/7